WALT DISNEY'S **Peter**

Random House 🏠 New York

Copyright © 1974 by Walt Disney Productions. All rights reserved under International and Pan-American Copyright Conventions. Published in the United States by Random House, Inc., New York, and simultaneously in Canada by Random House of Canada Limited, Toronto.
Library of Congress Cataloging in Publication Data
Disney (Walt) Productions.
Walt Disney's Peter and the wolf.
(Disney's wonderful world of reading, #20)
Retells Sergei Prokofiev's fairy tale of a Russian boy who captures a wolf with the help of a bird, duck and cat.
[1. Fairy tales] I. Title: Peter and the wolf. PZ8.D632Pe5 [E] 74-6423
ISBN 0-394-82563-2 ISBN 0-394-92563-7 (lib. bdg.)
Manufactured in the United States of America

OPQRSTUV 67890

Once there was a boy named Peter.
He lived with his Grandfather
near a big forest in Russia.
One day Peter was helping Grandfather.
Grandfather was chopping wood.
Peter was putting it into a pile.

When they were done, Peter said,
"May I go into the forest to play now?"
"Oh, no, Peter!" said Grandfather.
"You must stay away from the forest."

That night Peter asked,
"Why must I stay away from the forest?"
"It is winter now," said Grandfather.
"The forest is full of hungry wolves."
"I'm not afraid of wolves," said Peter.

The next morning Peter got up early.
Grandfather was still sleeping.
Peter took his toy gun and some rope.
He tiptoed past Grandfather's bed.
He sneaked out of the house.

"I'm going to catch me a wolf," said Peter.
And he went into the forest.
"After I catch him, I will shoot him —

like this!"
cried Peter.
"POW! POW!"

"Who is making
so much noise?"
asked Sasha the bird.

"It's me," said Peter.
"I was pretending to shoot a wolf."
"This is no place to pretend,"
said Sasha. "There are real wolves
in this forest."

"And I'm going to catch one," said Peter.
Sasha hopped onto Peter's gun.
"You will never catch a real wolf
with this toy gun," he said.

"I can try," said Peter.

"You might need help," said Sasha.

"Then come along," said Peter.

And off they went.

But suddenly
they stopped.
There before
them was a
big dark shadow!

"I think it's a wolf!"
whispered Peter.
Was Peter right?
Was it a wolf?

No!

It was Sonia the duck.

"Hi!" she said. "What are you doing here?"

"We are hunting for wolves," said Peter.

"Oh, let me hunt, too!" cried Sonia.

"I have always wanted to catch a wolf."

"Come along," said Peter.

And off they went.

They did not know that someone
was watching Sasha.
It was Ivan the cat.
And he was hungry.

No one saw Ivan sneak up behind Sasha.
"What a tasty breakfast!" Ivan thought.
No one saw Ivan put out his paw.

But when Ivan pounced and Sasha screeched,
everyone turned around.

"Ivan!" said Peter. "Give me that bird!"
Poor Ivan was so hungry.
Still, he let go of Sasha and looked sorry.

Then Ivan saw something
that made him jump.
He jumped so high
he landed on Peter's head.
"Look!" he cried. "A wolf!"

It WAS a wolf—a big, hungry wolf!
Everyone tried to hide behind a tree.
But the wolf came closer and closer.
They could see his sharp teeth
and his bright pink tongue.

Peter and Ivan climbed up the tree.
Sasha flew up beside them.
But Sonia could not climb OR fly.
"Run!" yelled Peter.
Sonia ran as fast as she could.
The wolf chased her into some bushes.

Then the wolf came out of the bushes.
He had a duck feather in his mouth.
Sonia did not come out.

Peter and his friends felt very sad.

"Poor Sonia," they said.

And they began to cry.

But there was no time for tears.
The wolf was trying to get up the tree.
Peter thought of a plan.
He told the plan to Sasha and Ivan.

Sasha flew down to tease the wolf.
The wolf tried to catch Sasha.
The wolf was so busy he did not
see Ivan put the rope around his tail.

Peter pulled the rope tight.
"Hurry, Ivan!" he cried.
"Help me pull the wolf up."

The wolf knew he was caught.
He began to kick and fight.

Then Peter and Ivan jumped off the branch.
The wolf went up into the air.

Peter held onto the rope.
Ivan held onto Peter.
"I'll go and get help," said Sasha.
And off he flew.

Sasha went through the forest
looking everywhere for help.

At last he saw three hunters.

The hunters were hunting for a wolf.

"This way!" cried Sasha. "Follow me."

But the hunters kept going.

They did not understand him.

Sasha flew down in front of the hunters.
He chirped as loudly as he could.
The hunters stood there looking at Sasha.
They still did not understand him.

Then Sasha had an idea.

He used his feet to make four letters in the snow—H-E-L-P.

"Now I understand," said one hunter. "We must follow this bird."

The hunters followed Sasha.
He led them to Peter and Ivan.
What a surprise for the hunters!
Peter and Ivan had caught a wolf.

"I'll kill that mean wolf," said a hunter.

"Oh, no!" cried Peter. "Don't kill him.
He isn't mean. He is just hungry.
Let's take him to the zoo."

"That is a good idea," said the hunters.

"The wolf can't be too hungry," said Sasha.
"He just had Sonia for breakfast."

"He did not!" said someone.
It was Sonia!

"Sonia! You are safe!" cried her friends.

Then everyone marched off to the zoo.
What a parade!
Peter and his friends led the way.
The hunters carried the wolf.

Soon they passed Peter's house.
When Grandfather saw the parade,
he could not believe his eyes.
Peter and his friends had caught a wolf!